Poptropica®

SKULLDUGGERY ISLAND

POPTROPICA

Published by the Penguin Group

Penguin Group (USA) Inc., 375 Hudson Street, New York, New York 10014, USA

Penguin Group (Canada), 90 Eglinton Avenue East, Suite 700,
Toronto, Ontario M4P 2Y3, Canada
(a division of Pearson Penguin Canada Inc.)

Penguin Books Ltd, 80 Strand, London WC2R 0RL, England

Penguin Ireland, 25 St Stephen's Green, Dublin 2, Ireland
(a division of Penguin Books Ltd)

Penguin Group (Australia), 707 Collins Street, Melbourne, Victoria 3008, Australia
(a division of Pearson Australia Group Pty Ltd)

Penguin Books India Pvt Ltd, 11 Community Centre,
Panchsheel Park, New Delhi—110 017, India

Penguin Group (NZ), 67 Apollo Drive, Rosedale, Auckland 0632, New Zealand
(a division of Pearson New Zealand Ltd)

Penguin Books, Rosebank Office Park,
181 Jan Smuts Avenue, Parktown North 2193, South Africa

Penguin China, B7 Jaiming Center, 27 East Third Ring Road North,
Chaoyang District, Beijing 100020, China

Penguin Books Ltd, Registered Offices: 80 Strand, London WC2R 0RL, England

ISBN 978-0-448-46200-4   10 9 8 7 6 5 4 3 2 1

SKULLDUGGERY
ISLAND

adapted by Adrianne Ambrose
cover illustrated by Angel Rodriguez
illustrated by The Artifact Group

Poptropica
An Imprint of Penguin Group (USA) Inc.

Chapter One

Homecoming

"Ahoy there, mateys," Owen Christopher said as he peered through a spyglass toward the port town of Fort Ridley. In the distance, he could barely make out the buildings of his hometown through the thick black clouds that filled the sky.

It had been months since he had signed on as cabin boy of the zeppelin *Aurora*, and Owen was feeling a bit homesick. Seeing that they were scheduled to pass by his home of Fort Ridley, he had put in for shore leave—or, more accurately, land leave, as the *Aurora* spent all its time soaring through the skies.

"Are you sure you want this time off?" Captain Arthur McCrea asked. "Fort Ridley looks to be a bit . . ." McCrea hunted for the right words. "Down at the boot heels."

Owen leaned over the side of the bow as the airship approached the edge of the black clouds. "That's smoke," he said. "I thought there was a storm brewing."

"Smells like gunpowder to me," McCrea added. "Someone's been firing off cannons."

"I can't see anyone down there," Owen said. "And it doesn't look like there are any ships in port. I wonder what happened to the navy."

Captain McCrea pointed farther out into the harbor. "There's one ship down there. And she's flying the Jolly Roger."

"Pirates?" Owen asked. "There haven't been pirates in Fort Ridley since before I was born. Quick, let's get to the port. I have to find out what's going on."

"I can't take the *Aurora* through that smoke cloud," McCrea said. "We're not getting anywhere near that port."

"But, sir," Owen pleaded. "That's my home. I have to get down there."

McCrea puffed out his chest and placed his hands on the ship's iron railing. After a moment he shook his head and let out a small sigh.

"Okay," the captain relented. "I can make a quick pass over the pier, but we can't stick around. Once you're out, you're out."

"I understand," Owen replied. He was anxious to get down to Fort Ridley.

"There's just one more thing," McCrea added. "And you're probably not going to like it . . ."

McCrea was right, Owen thought as he shinnied down a long stretch of rope and into the dark black smoke cloud. *I don't like this one bit.* He could hear the wind whipping past him as the *Aurora* made its descent into the skies above Fort Ridley. The zeppelin would only be able to stay in the cloud for a few moments, so Owen had to be ready to let go of the end of the rope and jump off as soon as they were over the piers.

Owen held his breath to avoid inhaling the soot from the cloud as he lowered himself down, one hand after another. He couldn't make out the docks or even the end of the rope.

"All right, son," McCrea called out from above. "It's now or never."

Below him, Owen saw only darkness mixed with the occasional swirl of grayish light. He tried to focus on something. Anything. For a brief moment, he thought he saw the wooden planks of the pier below his feet. Knowing this was his only chance, he let go of the rope.

Owen fell through the darkness for all of two seconds before his feet smacked against the pier, and he tumbled to the ground. Safely under the smoke cloud, Owen took a deep breath and stood up. Solid ground at last.

As he made his way down the pier and into the port, Owen couldn't help but be shocked at the state of the buildings. When he'd left, Fort Ridley had been booming. The market had been overflowing with freshly caught fish and exotic produce brought in from other islands. There were people everywhere, and kids played in the streets.

"Hey, you," a gruff voice called out. "You know you're not supposed to be in the port. It's too dangerous."

"What do you mean?" Owen asked the rough-looking soldier standing guard. "Where is everybody? And what's with the smoke? Has there been a fire?"

The soldier gave Owen a surprised look. "Are you new to these parts?" he asked.

"Not really," Owen told him. "I grew up here, but I've been away."

"What's your name?" the soldier inquired.

"Owen Christopher," was the reply.

"Well, Owen Christopher, the governor has told people to stay in their homes and avoid the port . . . at least until that blackheart Captain Crawfish is taken care of."

"Is Captain Crawfish that pirate who's anchored out in the harbor?" Owen asked. "Where's the navy? Why haven't they stopped him?"

"They tried," the soldier said. "We all did. But that pirate sank all our ships and sent cannonballs through most of the port. The navy's all but gone, and there's only a few of us soldiers left to protect the town. Look, kid, you better get home to your family. It isn't safe around here."

Owen thanked the soldier for the information and headed away from the port and into town. But before he left, he thought he'd check out that pirate ship. He made his way to the signal tower, where he knew he could get a full view of the harbor. As he made his way to the top, he was surprised to see an old sailor sitting there.

"Ahoy," Owen said. "I didn't think I'd find anyone up here."

"Just keeping watch," the old salt replied. "The same as always. Not that there's much need these days. I'm pretty much all that's left of the navy."

"Where did that pirate come from?" Owen asked.

"No one knows. He just showed up one night and started blasting holes in all the ships. Most of the navy was at the bottom of the harbor before we could ring the alarm. We tried holding him off, but without Captain Christopher to lead us, we never stood a chance."

Owen's heart sank. Captain Christopher was his father and the former commander of the local navy. Right after Owen left on the *Aurora*, his father quit the navy and took Owen's mother as far away from Fort Ridley as he could.

Grabbing the telescope mounted at the top of the tower, Owen pointed it toward the water.

Squinting into the lens, he scanned the horizon until he found what he was looking for: a large menacing ship with tall sails and a flag with the skull and crossbones at the top of its center mast.

Chapter Two

Old Friends

Back on the ground, Owen headed farther into Fort Ridley, looking for friends or at least familiar faces. From what he could tell, the rest of town looked just as bad as the docks. Many of the buildings had been knocked to the ground, and those that still stood had shattered windows and holes in their roofs. It seemed like most people had abandoned Fort Ridley.

Just then Owen heard yelling coming from down the road. He ran toward the commotion. As he approached the general store he saw two scruffy-looking pirates, carrying bags of feed over their shoulders, sprint out the door and down a side alley.

"If I ever get my hands on you, you rapscallions," an older woman yelled as she lumbered out the door of the store, waving a broom over her head, "I'll make you sorry you ever stepped foot in my store!"

As Owen ran up to the general store, he could see the empty shelves. Gone were the foodstuffs and bolts of fine fabric. The shelves and racks and display cases were empty—there was nothing to buy. No books, no spices, no swords—nothing.

The old shopkeeper sat down on the front steps. Her face lit up slightly when she saw Owen coming toward her. "Owen, am I glad to see your face. I sure hope you brought your father with you. That horrible Captain Crawfish has stolen everything we had. And he's blocked new goods from coming into port."

"I'm sorry, Mrs. Gilworth," Owen said. "I'm on my own. I haven't talked to my father in almost six months. Are you all right?"

"I'm fine. They won't be back. There's nothing left to take. That's too bad about your father, though. No one's been able to stop these attacks," the shopkeeper added. "And unless someone finds a way to bring merchants back to our port, we'll starve."

Owen sat with Mrs. Gilworth for a while and tried to convince her that everything was going to be all right—although he hardly believed it himself.

After leaving the general store, Owen headed farther into town. Eventually he came upon a bridge spanning a narrow waterway. At the far end stood a girl looking over the side, staring deep into the water.

"Hi, Matilda," he said, walking up to her.

"Owen," she said, a bit surprised. "Hi. I didn't know you were back in town."

"I just got here," he said. "I can't believe the state of things."

"I know. It's a huge mess. The town's barely holding on."

"I'm surprised to see you out here," Owen added. "This is hardly the place for the governor's daughter. I assumed he'd have you locked up in his mansion."

Matilda blushed. "As far as he knows I'm still under lock and key. I've been sneaking out of that house since we were little kids."

"I remember," Owen said. A slight smile crept across his face. It was the first time he'd smiled since coming home. "So, what does your father plan on doing about this pirate?"

"I don't know for certain. My father and old Captain MacCullen are hatching some kind of plan. He won't tell me too much about it because he's afraid I'll run off to join the fight."

"You always were the best sailor at school. Even better than me," Owen admitted.

"My father says that becoming a sailor is no life for a lady." She wrinkled her nose. "He wants me to become governor after he retires."

"Then we better make sure that there's still a town for you to govern."

"Why don't you come over for dinner tonight?" Matilda suggested. "We still have a little food. I'm sure my father will be happy to see you. He's looking for all the able men he can find. Just don't tell him you saw me running about town."

"You have my word," he told her. "But I need to go home first. If there's anything left of it."

"Don't get your hopes up. Those pirates

have taken everything that they could carry and destroyed the rest."

Owen nodded. "Even so, I feel that I need to see it."

Owen headed off toward his family home. It was an old house not too far off the main street. The Christophers had lived there for as far back as anyone in town could remember. As a little boy, Owen was told stories of Captain Nathaniel Christopher, who had commanded the first ship that settled Fort Ridley. Back then, the waters were filled with all kinds of giant sea monsters and pirates ten times worse than Captain Crawfish, according to family legend.

Owen was always told that he'd grow up to become a captain like all the Christopher men. But he never wanted that. He always had his eyes fixed on the sky and not the sea. And when the chance came for him to join the *Aurora*, he jumped at it.

His father retired from the navy not long afterward. Owen's mother confessed in a letter that his heart wasn't in it after Owen broke the family tradition. That's when his parents set off on a trip around the world. It felt horrible to disappoint his father, but Owen also knew that he had to pursue what he wanted from life.

As Owen looked at the remains of his family home—smashed windows, broken doors, and empty drawers and cupboards—he couldn't help but wonder: If he'd stayed and joined the navy, would his father have been able to stop Captain Crawfish? Was this all his fault?

Owen pushed through the debris and made his way over to an old bookcase, its contents scattered across the floor. He let out a relieved sigh as he reached up and pressed a secret latch hidden above the top shelf. *The pirates didn't find it*, he said to himself. The bookcase swung back and revealed a small room full of naval gear.

This secret room had been built in the early days of Fort Ridley as a safe room to protect the Christopher family from invading pirates and marauders. Years later, it had been turned into a museum of sorts. Generations of naval uniforms, swords, maps,

captains' hats, telescopes, and other nautical gear filled the room from floor to ceiling.

Most important, though, was the Christopher cutlass. The sword was a gift from Governor Thaddeus Ridley, the founder of Fort Ridley, to Nathaniel Christopher upon his appointment as captain of the official navy. It was a beautiful

cutlass with an intricately engraved blade and a hilt wrapped in sharkskin. The blade had Owen's great-great-grandfather's name and the Christopher crest engraved in curling script on one side and a portion of an ornate compass with ships, islands, and longitudinal lines on the other. Every Christopher in succession had carried this sword with them off to sea—except Owen.

Pleased that the room had been untouched, Owen closed the door, leaving his family's treasures in place. He straightened his clothes and tried to tame his wild hair. He wanted to look his best for dinner with the governor.

Chapter Three

The Secret Letter

Owen headed toward the center of town. The governor's mansion sat atop a small but steep hill that overlooked all of Fort Ridley. The hilltop was the site of the original Fort Ridley—a small protected compound that housed the eighty-seven original settlers. They found the highest and most secure location to build their town. Over the years, the town had spread both to the water's edge and off into the countryside.

A monument to Governor Thaddeus Ridley sat just to the north of the mansion. Owen stood in front of it and looked out to see the sun setting on Fort Ridley. Despite all the chaos and destruction, the golden beams of light dancing across the town's silhouetted buildings was still one of the most beautiful things he'd ever seen.

The mansion itself was in serious need of

repair, with large cracks in the walls and a few broken windows that had been boarded over. Owen climbed the steps of the front porch and knocked on the door. After a moment he heard the sound of several heavy locks releasing, and the door swung open. A slight man with thick, glossy hair and fine-looking clothes greeted him.

"Owen Christopher to see the governor," Owen said, trying to sound as grown-up as he could.

From inside the mansion, Owen heard a voice call out, "We're in the office."

Owen followed the slight man inside. In the center of what Owen assumed was the office, he saw two men examining a piece of very old paper.

"Owen, my boy, so good to see you," Governor Roland said, looking up. He had gray stubble sprouting from his cheeks and was wearing a tricorne hat. "How's the air service been treating you?"

"Fine, sir," Owen replied.

"Good. Good. I see you've met my aide and trusted friend, Jeeves," he said, gesturing to the slight man. Owen nodded and received a nod of recognition in return.

"And this is Captain MacCullen," the governor added, gesturing to the third man, who was significantly older than the governor. He had a weathered face, probably from years at sea, but his posture was ramrod straight. "He's volunteered to come out of retirement to lead what's left of our navy," the governor added.

"Aye. We only have one ship, and it's a rusted-out barge," the gruff old captain said. "I'd hardly call that a navy."

"We are grateful, anyway," the governor replied. "Captain, this is Owen Christopher, he's—"

"I know who this wee lad is," the captain barked. He fixed his eyes on Owen. "And let me just say, it's a right terrible thing you did, taking off like that. Your old father was never the same after you left."

Owen felt his face flush. It wasn't fair that people were always judging him against his father and grandfather and all the other Christophers. It wasn't fair that he was expected to join the navy just because they had all done it.

"It's a shame his father isn't here now," Jeeves said. "We really need a man of his caliber to fight Captain Crawfish."

"We've sent carrier pigeons off to find him," the governor said. "But even if he gets our message, I don't know what he could do to help."

Owen tried to ignore MacCullen's glare. "There must be something that the town can do for itself. Isn't there?" Owen asked.

"There is something," Governor Roland said in a slightly hushed tone. "A system that was put in place for defending the port that goes back generations."

"I would say that it's more of a legend than anything else," Jeeves added. "A folktale, that's all. Nothing more."

"It's more than that," Governor Roland said, pointing toward the old piece of paper on the table. "This document has been passed down from one governor to the next. This is what will save us."

"What is it?" Owen took a few steps closer to get a better look.

The governor's eyes widened as he read and then spoke in a half whisper. "It contains clues to the whereabouts of a treasure map!"

"Our town is in possession of a great treasure," MacCullen added. "But the only person who knew its location was buried long ago."

"But how will treasure stop the pirates?" Owen asked. "Is it some kind of magic cannonball or something?"

"Nothing as fanciful as that, laddie," the captain grumbled. "It's enough gold and jewels to hire the biggest and best naval fleet that money can buy."

"Captain MacCullen is going to lead an expedition to find the map and the treasure," the governor explained. "Meanwhile, Jeeves is heading off to Golden Harbor to make the arrangements to secure a fleet to defeat that dread pirate, Crawfish."

"But first we need to decode this letter and find the location of the map," Jeeves said.

Owen stepped right up next to the men and looked at the document.

Ever since the legendary pirate Captain Keelhaul and his crew were driven from our waters, I've dreaded the day when a new marauder might target our prosperous home. That is why I have hidden our town's vast fortune where no pirate will ever look for it. Only I know the treasure's whereabouts, and it's my duty to keep it safe.

And so, on this fifth day of October, I have drawn up a map to the treasure, and divided it into five parts. I have sent the pieces to the neighboring islands and have asked trusted friends to hide their portions from prying eyes.

But just to be sure that the treasure isn't lost to time, even if many years have passed, here are some clues that will help those with a true heart and a clear mind:

Parrot Port

~Birds of a feather guard the vast treasure. If you're ever at such a port of call, you'll have to make a feathered friend if you want any treasure at all.

Pirate Outpost

~Even pirates must brush their teeth, or their days will end in grief. No matter how you fill your hold, a beautiful smile is worth its weight in gold.

Golden Harbor

~Golden lights twinkle in the night.
Just make sure you're safe and get the
combination right.

Dragon Cove

~You can always make a wish on a fish,
but you're not alone if you find your
destiny carved in stone.

Bouffant Bay

~When ferns are your passion, you'll
find you're in fashion. If things get too
hot, you've found the right spot.

Only when all the pirates are
vanquished and our waters are cleared of
danger should the pieces of the map be
brought back together and the treasure
returned to our humble island.

I am growing old, and my days on this earth are numbered. I can only hope the person who holds this document is good and true and will do what's best for the people of my beloved island.

Governor Ridley

"But this document must be very old," Owen said when he was finished reading. "I'm sure whoever was trusted with the pieces of the map is long gone by now."

"There's only one way to find out. That's why we have to decipher the clues and hunt down the treasure so we can hire a navy," Jeeves said, jabbing a finger at the paper. "And fast."

Owen wasn't convinced. "It says right at the bottom that we shouldn't seek the treasure until we get rid of the pirates."

The governor shook his head. "There was no way they could have known back then the suffering our community would face due to Captain Crawfish. The treasure was meant to be used for an emergency, and this is definitely an emergency."

Owen shrugged. "I guess you're right."

"Now come on," the governor said as he rolled up the letter and put it back into his safe. "Let's all enjoy one final meal together. Who knows if we'll ever have this chance again?"

Chapter Four

Set Sail for Adventure

They were joined for dinner by Matilda, who gave Owen a sly, knowing wink, and her mother, the governor's wife. They ate a simple meal of fish and bread, and nobody spoke of pirates— although it was clear that all Matilda wanted to do was talk about them.

After dinner, Owen found Captain MacCullen staring out of a window and looking toward the sea. "That's the only place I've ever wanted to be: the water," the captain said. "But you wouldn't know anything about that, now would you?"

Owen felt a little uncomfortable. "Look," he said. "I know you don't like me, but I can be a help. I know my way around a ship. I want to join your crew."

"Ha!" MacCullen laughed. "You might know your way around one of those fancy flying ships, but you are by no means a sailor. If we weren't so desperate for a crew, I'd tell you to take a long walk off a short pier." The old man turned to rejoin the gathering, but before he did, he glanced over his shoulder at Owen and snapped, "We leave at sunrise. Don't be late."

After he left the governor's mansion, Owen headed back down to what was left of his home. He lit whatever candles and lanterns he could find and began to clean up as best he could. In the debris he found old family pictures and keepsakes. He placed them carefully into neat piles as he swept broken glass and shards of wood out the front door.

Just after midnight, he went to the bookcase and unlatched the secret door. If he was going to head out to sea on his first—and perhaps final—voyage, there was something that he needed by his side. As he lifted the Christopher cutlass, he felt immediately aware of its weight. He'd held the sword many times as a boy, but he never realized how heavy it was. Perhaps he could feel the weight of all the past Christophers on his shoulders: their combined history. *Was this what my father felt?* he wondered. *Was this why he became a captain?*

The next morning, Owen made his way onto the docks, the cutlass secured to his side, just as the sun first showed itself in the sky.

Owen was surprised to see Captain MacCullen standing on the dock next to an old, rusting barge. He had assumed the captain had been exaggerating about the only boat left on the island, but he obviously wasn't. There were a few townsfolk standing around the dock, mostly farmers, as far as Owen could tell. There was even a boy much younger than Owen with what appeared to be a wooden sword, and the old sailor from the top of the tower. MacCullen really was recruiting every able-bodied person left in port.

"Listen up, men," the captain began. "And

women," he added, in consideration of a few women who had also volunteered for service. "We have our orders, and I won't lie to you, it's pretty grim. We've only got this"—he gestured toward the barge—"um . . . vessel at our disposal. I'm afraid she isn't very fast, and she has no cannons."

"What be her name?" the old sailor ventured to ask. "Any ship, no matter how rundown, should have a proper name."

"Her name?" The captain looked a little flummoxed. "Ermmm . . ." He eyed the barge warily.

"How about *The Guppy*?" the boy suggested, causing some small chuckles from the makeshift crew.

"Ah," the old sailor said. "*The Guppy* be a fine name for such a boat. It suits her."

"Fine," the captain agreed. He obviously felt the name of the boat was of little importance. "But let's get down to what really matters. Our mission is to avoid Captain Crawfish at all costs. We must search every island in our archipelago for the pieces of a missing map. Then, once we have the map, we will search for the treasure."

"What treasure?" the young boy asked.

"A vast treasure that will save our town from ruin; that's all you need to know," the captain snapped. "Captain Crawfish is a ruthless scourge of the seas, and this is a dangerous expedition, so anyone having second thoughts should leave now." He glared at them all, his eyes narrowed to slits.

"Of course, you'll always be labeled a coward from here on out, but don't let that stop you." The captain waited several seconds, but nobody moved. "Good," he said. "Now line up and sound off. Tell me who you are and what you think you can do aboard our ship to help the cause."

"I'm called Bilge, Captain," the old sailor said, stepping forward first. "And I've been a cook on many a voyage."

"I see," the captain replied. It was obvious he would have preferred someone with knowledge of navigation, but he was forced to take whatever crew he could get. "Welcome to the crew, Bilge."

Next was the young boy. He piped up with, "I'm William Winslow, but I'm called Billy."

"And what do you propose to do with that wooden sword?" the captain asked with an amused tone.

Billy furrowed his brow. "Well, I aim to fight Captain Crawfish."

MacCullen chuckled. "At least you got heart, lad. Welcome aboard. You can be a cabin boy for now."

The introductions went on down the line until it was Owen's turn, as he stood at the end. "I'm Owen Christopher," he said, keeping his voice firm and steady. "I've never been to sea, but I've been to air for six months as a cabin boy on the *Aurora*. I'm a quick study, and I can do whatever you assign me."

Owen wasn't sure what MacCullen was going to say, but the captain just gave him a solemn nod. "Okay, men and women, let's launch *The Guppy* and be on our way."

They were just about to board when they saw the governor and Jeeves coming down the dock. "Safe voyage," Governor Roland called. "We all look forward to your speedy return."

36

"Thank you, Governor," MacCullen replied as he saluted.

"Where are you headed?" Jeeves asked. "Where will you start this treasure hunt?"

"Dragon Cove," the captain answered with conviction. "Once we weigh anchor we'll be on our way."

"I'm sure you don't need it, but I had Jeeves scrounge you up a map of the region," the governor said, giving his trusted servant a nudge. Jeeves felt inside his breast pocket and pulled out a rolled map.

"Much appreciated, Governor," MacCullen said with a short bow. "But now we must be going." With that, he stepped aboard *The Guppy*, and the ship launched.

Owen was a little confused by the route the captain ordered to Dragon Cove. He wasn't a sailor, but their course really didn't make sense to him. Still, he thought it was best not to question the captain.

The barge was as slow moving a boat as Owen could imagine. *In fact*, he thought, *if it goes any slower we'll be standing still.* After about an hour in the water, Billy jumped up and pointed out into the water. "Hey! There's a raft out there."

The crew turned to look, and sure enough, there was a small raft headed in their direction and gaining on them. The captain used his spyglass to see who was approaching. "It's a girl," he said aloud, but with some confusion. "Why would she be out here all alone?"

"Oh." Something occurred to Owen. "Captain, do you mind if I borrow your spyglass? I think I might know who that is."

Training the spyglass on the small vessel, Owen focused on the raft. His suspicions were correct. "I know her!" he exclaimed. "It's Matilda, the governor's daughter."

MacCullen gave orders to slow the barge, which wasn't difficult to do, and Matilda caught up with them in no time. "What are you doing here?" Owen asked as the girl hopped aboard the ship. She was dressed like a sailor and had a small knapsack with her.

"I've come to volunteer," she explained.

"Well, why didn't you just do that at the dock, like a normal person?" Owen asked.

The girl lowered her voice so only Owen could hear. "You know my father would never let me. I had to sneak out."

"Turn *The Guppy* around," MacCullen commanded. "We have to return the governor's daughter to port."

"You can't," Matilda insisted. "We're too far out. It would cause a huge delay in our mission."

The captain looked uncertain, so the girl quickly added, "Besides, I'm an excellent sailor, and I'm ready to fight Captain Crawfish wherever he rears his ugly head."

"Captain Crawfish!" Billy shouted.

"That's right," Matilda said to him.

"No, you don't understand," the boy insisted. "Look!" He pointed out at the water.

Sure enough, it was the same pirate ship that Owen had seen anchored off the coast of Fort Ridley.

Chapter Five

Ambush

"Full speed ahead," Captain MacCullen yelled to the crew. "Let's see what this bucket of rust can do."

"You're seeing it now, Captain. We're going as fast as we can," one of the crew members replied.

Owen and Matilda watched as the giant pirate ship tore through the water toward them.

"How did he find us so quickly?" Bilge wondered. "It's almost like the scurvy dog knew where we'd be."

"We have to get out of here!" Billy exclaimed.

"No." The captain stuck out his chin. "If we can't outrun them, we will fight them."

"Captain, you can't be serious," Owen replied. "That ship destroyed our entire navy. We don't even have a cannon. Do you expect us to fight them off with wooden swords?"

"What would you do then?" MacCullen barked.

"I don't know. But it's foolish to stand and fight when there's no chance we'll survive," Owen pointed out. "The best thing we can do is try to get to Dragon Cove before they catch us. If we make it to shallow enough water, that big ship won't be able to follow."

Captain MacCullen grumbled something to himself as he looked at Dragon Cove in the distance and then back at the pirate ship speeding toward them.

"We need to find the pieces of the map," Owen added. "That's our mission. Not fighting Crawfish."

"Fine," MacCullen growled. Although it annoyed him, he knew that Owen was right. "Let's get this boat to Dragon Cove as quick as we can. Paddle with ye hands if you think it will help."

"We need to arm ourselves, just in case," Matilda said to Owen.

"I have my cutlass, and the captain has a sword," Owen said. "But is there anything at all useful on this barge? Besides Billy's wooden sword."

They scrambled around, looking for anything they could use to defend themselves. "Bilge can use his frying pan," Matilda said. "And I found these short planks of wood used for decking, which the other sailors can use as clubs."

"What about you?" Owen asked. He hadn't found anything he thought was useful.

"I found this length of rope that I can use as a whip, and I brought my rapier," she told him.

"That's fine for dueling," Owen said. "But it isn't exactly the sword of choice for facing marauding pirates."

"Don't worry. I'm pretty good with this thing." She pulled the long, thin sword from her gear and sliced it through the air a couple of times. "I'll be fine."

"They be closing in on us!" Bilge called out.

Owen grabbed the spyglass and aimed it at the pirate ship. On its deck, he could see a sinister-looking man with a shocking crimson hat. As the pirate turned his grizzled head, Owen saw that he had an eye patch with a skull and crossbones. *That must be Captain Crawfish*, he said to himself. *No one else could look that evil.*

"Do you think we're going to make it to shore, Captain?" Matilda asked. "That ship is getting awful close."

"Not a chance," MacCullen replied as he

drew his sword. "Grab whatever you can use as a weapon. Looks like it's going to be a fight after all."

Owen and Matilda stood with their swords ready as the giant pirate ship pulled up next to *The Guppy*. They could hear the pirates calling out orders to each other. It would only be seconds until they boarded the barge.

The pirates climbed over the side of their ship and swung down on ropes to the deck of *The Guppy*. "Repel all boarders!" MacCullen ordered, but there was little his ragtag crew could do as the barge filled with pirates brandishing swords and clenching daggers in their teeth.

"Let me at them," Billy called out as he waved his wooden sword in the air. He charged at the oncoming invaders, but before he could reach them a pirate swinging on a rope kicked him square in the chest. The young boy went flying through the air and landed in the sea with a wail and a splash.

"I'll save you," Bilge said, grabbing the barge's only life preserver and preparing to jump over the side as well.

"There's no time for that," Owen told the old

salt, while fending off a pirate with his cutlass. "Just throw him the preserver and keep fighting."

The old sailor scoffed. "I'm a cook," he said as if it was the most obvious thing in the world. "I don't fight. I boil, I fry, I maybe even bake, but I don't fight." With that, Bilge leaped over the side and was in the water paddling toward the sputtering Billy.

"Look out!" Matilda shouted. A large pirate with a long scar across his cheek was lunging toward Owen, his large cutlass raised in the air. Matilda managed to divert the blow with her rapier, but the force was too much for her slender sword, and the blade broke in half. "Not good," she said, dropping the now-useless weapon.

Owen thrusted his cutlass at the scar-faced pirate, hoping to draw his attention from Matilda.

"Take that!" Matilda had tied a knot at the end of her piece of rope and was using it to whip the pirate's face.

"Ahh!" the pirate shrieked, shielding his eyes.

Matilda drew back her arm in anticipation of dealing the pirate another blow, not realizing that

Owen was standing so close behind her. "Watch it!" Owen barked as he, in turn, felt the sting of the rope.

"Sorry." Matilda tried to jerk the rope away from him. Unfortunately, it became tangled around Owen's sword-bearing arm. He pulled back, but his arm was caught. He couldn't move without losing his cutlass.

The scar-faced pirate moved in on Matilda and Owen. They struggled to untangle the rope, but there wasn't enough time. The pirate raised his sword and started to swing.

"Hold on tight and follow my lead," Owen said. "I have a plan."

Before Matilda could respond, Owen charged forward. "Go around the other side of him," he called out as he ducked and ran past the pirate. Matilda did the same on the other side. The pirate paused to figure out what was happening. Before he could think, the length of rope caught him across the stomach and pulled him backward.

Owen and Matilda kept running, dragging the pirate back and knocking him to the deck.

"We did it," Matilda cried out, but her celebration came too soon. As the scar-faced pirate fell, he sliced at the rope with his sword. As the rope split in two, Owen and Matilda were thrown forward. Before they could brace themselves, they both tumbled off the side of the barge.

"Quick, back on the boat," Owen called out as his head splashed out of the water.

"I don't think that's the best idea," Matilda replied as she came sputtering to the surface.

Owen looked up to the deck of *The Guppy* and saw MacCullen waving a white handkerchief in the air, surrendering the barge and crew to Crawfish.

"So what do we do now?" Matilda asked.

"Swim for Dragon Cove" was all Owen could think to suggest.

Chapter Six

Dangers of Pirate Outpost

The waves thrashed up against Matilda and Owen as they struggled against the current. Behind them, they could see Captain Crawfish's ship heading back out to sea. Ahead lay the distant shores of Dragon Cove. Dry land was a long way off, but a good swim was better than surrendering to the pirates.

As they made their way closer to the island, Owen thought he could hear a voice calling out.

"Do you hear that?" he yelled to Matilda, who was a little ahead of him. "I think someone's calling to us."

Matilda slowed down so Owen could catch up. "There it is again," Owen said. This time they both heard it.

"Ahoy!" the voice called out. In the distance they saw Bilge and Billy sharing the life preserver and kicking toward the same island.

"Ahoy, yourself," Owen replied as he and Matilda swam toward them.

It took well over an hour to reach the island. They took turns using the preserver so that no one got too tired. But the closer they got to land, the more apparent it became that they weren't approaching Dragon Cove. What they saw was a small steep island piled high with giant rocks. At the base sat a huge boulder that had been carved in the shape of a foreboding skull.

"This be bad," Bilge remarked. "That there's the Pirate Outpost, I'd bet me life on it. It's one of the roughest places in these parts."

Matilda gave Owen a concerned look. "How did we get way over here?" she asked. "Pirate Outpost is nowhere near Dragon Cove."

"Maybe Captain MacCullen isn't as good a navigator as he thought," Owen replied. "Let's get to shore, and we'll worry about getting to Dragon Cove later."

The sun was setting by the time they reached land. Their cold, wet clothes hung off their bodies as they made their way up the beach.

"The only thing on this island looks to be the outpost," Matilda said. "I say we head that way."

"That place gives me the creeps," Billy said, trying to shake off the water. "Pirates are scarier than I thought."

"Aye," Bilge agreed. "Pirate Outpost be a place of blackhearts and thieves. You can't trust pirates . . . although I've known a few who could cook up a mean casserole."

"Do you think we could hire a ship there?" Matilda asked.

"I don't want to go anywhere near that outpost," Billy added. "There has to be someone else on this island with a ship we can hire. I'd rather try to build a raft out of coconuts than go up there."

"No, there's a piece of the map in that outpost," Owen said as he gripped the hilt of the cutlass hanging from his side. "I've had it up to here with pirates, and I aim to collect it."

They made their way up the beach and along a winding, briar-filled trail that led to the outpost. Two giant thugs stood guard on either side of the only door leading into the rundown building.

"Only the worthy shall enter through these here doors," the first thug said.

"Argg. Are ye worthy?" the second thug added.

"Know ye the name of the one who calls the seafarers home?" the first thug asked. "From shore to reef and from dusk to dawn. Under the stars and . . ."

"Marigold," Bilge blurted out.

"Aye, a beautiful lass she is at that," the first thug said.

"In ya go," the second one added with a knowing nod as he opened the door.

Bilge nodded back as he made his way past the others and entered the outpost.

Owen, Matilda, and Billy gave him an odd look and followed.

"How did you figure that out?" Matilda asked.

"Figured nothin'," Bilge replied. "I said this place is rough; never said I ain't been here before. Have a great stroganoff special on Tuesdays, they do."

Owen's confidence dropped as he entered the Pirate Outpost. Until earlier that morning he'd never even seen a real-life pirate before. Now he stood in a room full of them. As the group entered the dingy tavern, all eyes fell upon them.

A menacing-looking pirate with a long gray beard rose out his seat and walked over to Owen. "This be a dangerous place. Too dangerous for the likes of you," the man hissed.

"The Tuesday crowd be a bit friendlier," Bilge added as he moved behind Owen.

As the bearded pirate opened his mouth, Owen noticed a dingy gold tooth.

Owen remembered what the governor's letter said: *Even pirates must brush their teeth, or their days will end in grief. No matter how you fill your hold, a beautiful smile is worth its weight in gold.*

"We're here to find something, and I think you might be able to help us," Owen said to the pirate. "Once we have it, we'll be leaving."

"Oh, you'll be leavin', all right," the pirate said. "On ye heads."

The room erupted in laughter as the other pirates rose and started moving toward Owen and the others.

"Come on, Owen," Matilda said as she tugged on his sleeve. "I don't think we're going to get any help here."

"But you don't understand," Owen pleaded to the pirate. "You're supposed to help us."

Before the pirate could respond, Matilda and Bilge dragged Owen from the outpost.

As they turned to run down the trail and back to the beach, they saw another group of gruff pirates heading their way. Behind them, they could hear the pirates from the tavern chasing after them.

Billy nervously pulled out his wooden sword.

"This really isn't how I thought the day was going to go."

The gold-toothed pirate stepped up to Owen. "You won't be leavin' without some kind of payment. How's about you hand over that fancy sword."

Owen looked down at his cutlass. There was no way he could hand it over to this pirate. His family had kept it safe for generations. He would have to fight his way out.

Before Owen could get his hand on the hilt of the cutlass, the pirate already had a dagger pointed at his throat.

"That was a big mistake," the pirate said. "Now you're going to pay with your lives."

"Relax, Larry," a gravelly female voice called out. All heads turned to see a woman with long wavy red hair stroll out of the shadows. "They're just kids and an old man. I'm sure they're not here to make trouble." She looked Owen straight in the eye. "Are you?"

"No," Owen stammered. "Our ship was captured by pirates, and we had to swim to shore.

We thought we were headed for Dragon Cove."

The woman smirked and gave a small laugh. "You're a long way from Dragon Cove."

"We've figured that out," Owen said as he looked at the dozens of pirates looming over them.

The woman glared at the other pirates. "All right, boys," she said. "You've had your fun. Leave these outsiders to me."

The pirate horde all looked to the gray-bearded pirate, who reluctantly nodded and headed back to the tavern. The others followed him.

"I'm Morgan," the woman said, extending her hand to Owen. She wore a long jacket and leather boots that folded over at the top.

"Owen," he said, shaking her hand with a firm grip.

"How are you planning on getting off this rock?" Morgan asked.

"I'm afraid we don't know," Owen admitted. "Try to hire a boat, I guess."

Morgan hiked an eyebrow. "I've got a ship. You've got the money to pay me?"

Owen stuck his hands in his pockets and felt

only a few small doubloons. "Not really." Owen shook his head. "But I'll be able to pay you soon. And, I mean, pay well."

She seemed intrigued. "What exactly do you mean by *pay well*? Do you mean as in some kind of reward or something?"

Owen was reluctant to mention their plans—or the word *treasure*—in front of her. He explained that they had several stops to make and once they were done, she'd get her payment.

Looking at her nails, Morgan said, "Well, I just happen to be free at the moment, so I suppose I could help you out. But whatever this reward is, it'd better be good."

"Oh, it will be," Owen assured her. "But before we agree to anything, what kind of ship do you have? Is it fast? The last vessel we were on was kind of slow moving."

Morgan also took note of the grumbling of the unfriendly locals. "If we have a deal, maybe we'd better sleep aboard my ship tonight. I know a little cove we can use that's out of the way. We can launch tomorrow at first light."

Chapter Seven

The Riddle of Dragon Cove

Morgan did indeed have a fast ship. Sleek and low to the water, *The Lark* seemed perfect for slipping in and out of a port without drawing much notice. She maintained a small crew, none of whom appeared all that eager to be social with Owen and the others.

"This doesn't look like a pirate ship," Owen said to Matilda as they sat in the back of *The Lark* and watched the crew hurry about.

"I know," she replied in a voice just above a whisper. "I think she might be a smuggler. I'd be willing to bet Morgan is a rumrunner. I've read books about them. I know they're outlaws, but there's something so glamorous about them."

"What do you think your father would do if you became a *rumrunner*?" Owen asked with a little laugh.

"He'd probably lock me away until I was an old lady," she replied. "It's not fair."

"Do you really want to be a smuggler?" Owen asked.

"No, but if I did, I should be able to," Matilda said. "I want to join the navy. If we stop Crawfish, they're going to need new sailors. And I'm just as able as anybody else."

"Maybe your father will let you once we get back."

"Ha!" Matilda replied. "I doubt he'll ever speak to me again."

The next morning, Morgan woke everyone at the crack of dawn. Owen and Matilda made their way to the deck as *The Lark* pulled into Dragon Cove.

"How's that for service?" Morgan smirked at Owen.

"I've never seen anything like this," Matilda said as she pointed at the large ornate dragon statues looming over the dock.

Dragon Cove was very different from Fort Ridley. Everywhere Owen looked, he saw statues carved out of stone, and red buildings with strange-looking peaked roofs. Even the people dressed differently; everyone wore brightly colored robes.

"I'm excited to look around," Owen said. "This is going be a real adventure."

"I'd be careful," Bilge added. "You never know what you'll find in strange lands."

"The old-timer's right," Morgan said. "You sure you don't want me to come along? I know this island like the back of my hand."

Owen did want Morgan's help; it would certainly make finding the map piece easier. But he wasn't sure he could trust her. The map pieces were the only things that could save Fort Ridley, and he couldn't risk anything happening to them.

"No, you should stay with the ship," Owen replied. "Matilda and I will be fine on our own. We shouldn't be too long."

Owen and Matilda debarked and headed down the docks and into town. *You can always make a wish on a fish, but you're not alone if you find your destiny carved in stone,* Owen kept repeating to himself.

"Where do you make a 'wish on a fish'?" Owen asked.

"Some kind of wishing well?" Matilda replied. "Or a pond? Can you see any of those things around here?"

"I'm guessing the 'carved in stone' part has something to do with these statues."

They looked around and saw plenty of dragon statues, but no wishing wells or ponds. And certainly no fish.

"This is no good," Owen said. "How are we supposed to solve this riddle if we can't even find a clue?"

"Maybe there's fish back at the water?" Matilda suggested.

"It can't hurt to look."

They made their way back to the waterfront. All they saw was an old man sitting on a crate, contemplating the waves and casting a net into the water.

"The fish just aren't biting today," the man said.

"Speaking of fish," Owen said. "Do you know anything about wishing wells or fish statues?"

"I don't know nothin' about wishing wells," the man said. "But there is a fish statue submerged just off the shore there."

Owen and Matilda looked to where the man pointed. About fifty yards off the shore was a small piece of stone poking up out of the water.

"That there's the tip of it," the man said. "No one knows what it's doing out there, but it's been there forever."

"I'm going to go check it out," Owen said as he ran into the water.

"Be careful," Matilda called after him.

"And don't scare away the fish!" the man added.

Owen waded into the cold water and then, once he was far enough out, dove in and started swimming toward the statue. His muscles still burned from swimming to shore the previous day.

Gripping the top of the statue, he pulled himself up. *It certainly looks like the mouth of a fish,* he thought. *But how do I find the map piece?* He took a deep breath and dove under the water. Below the surface of the water, Owen searched the massive fish statue for buttons or levers. He was sure there would be a secret compartment.

Owen pulled himself back up on the statue and thought about the clue: *You can always make a wish on a fish, but you're not alone if you find your destiny carved in stone.*

A wish on a fish, he kept repeating to himself. *How do you make a wish?*

"With a coin!" he called out. Owen examined the mouth of the fish and found a small slit the size of a coin. He reached into his pocket and pulled out a doubloon and inserted it into the slit.

The coin plunked down into the statue. Moments later, a machinelike sound came out of the fish's mouth. Then the statue began to shake and rise up out of the water. The vibration must have awoken all the fish in the area, because

suddenly dozens of fish started leaping out of the water all around the statue.

"Not good, not good, not good!" Owen yelped as he held on to the tip of the statue. The giant stone fish rose higher and higher until it finally came to a grinding halt. Owen steadied himself and started looking around for clues to the map's location. Just then the statue made another mechanical sound, and its mouth began to open up. There sat an old bottle with a cork stuck in the top. Inside was what looked like a rolled piece of paper.

Owen grabbed the bottle and, holding it tightly, started to climb down the statue. Once at its base, he dove back into the water and swam for land.

"I can't believe it!" Matilda shouted as Owen pulled himself to shore.

"I know!" the old man shouted back.

Owen and Matilda turned to see the man happily jumping up and down with a net overflowing with fish.

Chapter Eight

A Close Call at Golden Harbor

"How'd things go at Dragon Cove?" Morgan asked as Matilda and a sopping-wet Owen made their way up the gangplank to *The Lark*.

"Fine," Owen said. "Quite good, actually."

"Did you get what you came for?" Morgan asked as she spied the bottle that Owen clutched in his hands.

"Yes, I, uh . . .," Owen tried to reply without telling the smuggler what they'd found.

"Yes, we did," Matilda answered as she grabbed the bottle from Owen and headed belowdecks.

"Great," Morgan replied as she gave Matilda a suspicious look. "So, where are we off to next?"

"I reckon Golden Harbor is the closest," Bilge said as he poked his head out of the ship's galley.

He and Billy had been lending a hand to the crew of *The Lark*.

"Golden Harbor it is, then," Morgan replied. Then she ordered the crew to set sail.

"In some ways this reminds of the summers I would spend out in the water with my father," Owen said to Morgan, who was coiling a length of rope as Owen leaned against the rail. "He and I would take out this small boat and just sail around Fort Ridley. Some days we'd fish, others just talk or count the number of pelicans we saw."

"Are you still close with your father?" she asked.

"Not really," he said. "My heart was never in the sea. At some point we just ran out of things to talk about. Now he's off traveling around the world, and I don't know if I'll ever see him again."

"I know how you feel," Morgan said as she leaned on the railing next to him. "My family is still in Fort Ridley, both of my parents and my younger sister, but they don't agree with how I make my living. I send them money anytime I have a little extra, but I haven't been home in almost three years."

"How *do* you make your living, if you don't mind me asking?"

"It's no secret," she replied. "I take things from one place to another. I don't ask questions and I don't get caught."

"And you don't care what you transport?" Owen asked.

"Not as long as I'm getting paid," she answered with a smirk. "Speaking of which, when do you think I'll see some of that payment you promised me?"

"I thought you didn't ask questions," Owen replied, mirroring her smirk.

The Lark lived up to its reputation for speed, and they arrived at Golden Harbor in no time. The town's docks were a crazy bazaar full of exotic food stalls, and people selling pottery, strange clothes, and other colorful items.

"This is amazing," Owen said as the crew moored *The Lark* to the dock. "There are so many wonderful smells."

"Golden Harbor be known for its spices," Bilge said. "I might do a little shopping while we're here. As long as no one minds."

"Just stay close to the ship," Owen replied. "You never know when we'll need to leave."

Bilge grunted and made his way down the docks, Billy trailing him.

"And I suppose the two of you will be off on one of your secret missions again?" Morgan said to Owen and Matilda.

Owen blushed slightly, while Matilda gave the smuggler a hard stare. There was something about Morgan that she didn't trust.

"Just make sure the ship's ready to go when we get back," she said as she grabbed Owen's sleeve and heading off the ship.

"Okay," Matilda said once they were out of earshot of Morgan. "'Golden lights twinkle in the night. Just make sure you're safe and get the combination right.' What do you think it means?"

"Perhaps there are some lights that we can only see at night," he replied. "It's still day, so maybe we need to hang out until it gets dark."

"What about the other bit?" she asked. "Safes have combinations. Maybe that's what we should be looking for?"

Owen thought about it for a moment. "Banks have safes," he said. "Let's find a bank."

They strolled through the streets of the town until they came upon a building that looked like a castle. The sign out front read GOLDEN HARBOR BANK.

It was unlike any other bank Owen had ever seen. There were safes and coins and stacks of money everywhere. Situated around the room were several mean-looking guards dressed all in black and carrying big curved swords. One of the guards noticed Owen just glancing in the direction of a pile of gold and growled.

"Owen, look," Matilda said in a hushed voice. "Check out that safe."

He looked in the direction she was nodding. There was a giant safe with an intricately decorated metal door depicting the street scene right in front of the bank. Hanging above the safe were five decorative lamps all twinkling as if they were reflecting moonlight.

"That has got to be it," Matilda breathed.

They took half a step toward the safe and were immediately cut off by what seemed to be the biggest guard in the place. "What are you kids doing in here?" he snarled. "Do you have business with the bank?"

"Uh . . .," Owen tried to think. "We're here to make a withdrawal from our account. It's just in that safe over there."

"That safe?" the guard replied as if it was the craziest thing he had ever heard.

"Yeah," Matilda added. "We'll just grab our *withdrawal* and be on our way."

"There's nothing in that safe for you," the guard said as he moved closer to them. "This bank is no place for kids."

Just then two giant hands reached down and picked Owen and Matilda up by their collars. Before they could protest, the guard deposited them on the sidewalk outside the bank.

"Don't let me catch you two playing around here again," he growled one final time before closing the bank's door in their faces.

"Now what do we do?" Owen said. "How are we going to get into that safe?"

"I know exactly what we're going to do," Matilda answered. "We're going to disguise ourselves to get back in there, then find someplace to hide until the bank closes for the evening. After that, we'll have to figure out something."

"Do you think it'll work?"

"Do you have a better plan?"

Matilda led them back to the bazaar by the docks. Rummaging through all the stalls and shops, she found what she was looking for.

"I feel ridiculous," Owen said in a muffled voice as they headed back into the bank.

"Keep quiet," Matilda hissed. She was standing on his shoulders and had on a long black coat that covered both of them. She'd tucked her hair up into a plumed hat that she wore low over her eyes. "It'll look suspicious if I'm having a conversation with my belly button."

Although Owen couldn't see what they looked like, he was sure that they looked ridiculous. The bank guards would easily see that they weren't a tall man in a hat. Owen could barely walk straight, and he had no idea where he was going. Every time he tried to peer out of the jacket, they started to wobble.

Matilda did her best to guide him by kicking him and *gently* digging her heels into his shoulders. After a few minutes, she signaled him by stomping three times with her left foot. Owen dropped to the floor as quietly as he could as Matilda slid out of the jacket. He looked over the pile of gold they were hiding behind and couldn't see anyone looking at them. Their plan was working.

Once Matilda was out of the jacket she unfolded a big piece of shiny gold fabric and covered them with it. Hopefully no one would spot them before the bank closed.

They waited quietly for several minutes after the lights went out and they heard the doors lock from the outside. "Now to figure out the safe's combination," Owen said as he poked his head out from under the gold fabric.

Owen and Matilda both stared at the door of the giant safe and tried to figure out the clue. *Golden lights twinkle in the night. Just make sure you're safe and get the combination right.*

Finally, Owen whispered, "I think I have it. Look at the street scene decorating the door. There are five streetlamps, but only three of the lamps are lit: the first, the second, and the fourth. Maybe that's the safe's combination."

"Try it." Matilda shrugged.

Owen sidled up to the giant safe's dial and tentatively spun it right, then left, then right, using the numbers one, two, and four. Nothing happened. Then he tried two, four, and one. Still no luck. "This isn't working," he said with a sigh.

Matilda rubbed her chin and looked at the design on the safe's door some more, then glanced up at the lamps hanging above the safe. "Maybe the map piece isn't actually in the safe. Maybe the clue has more to do with these lamps." She tapped Owen on the arm. "Give me a boost."

With Owen staggering as he lifted her, Matilda tried switching on the different lamps hanging above the safe. She tried different variations of the first, second, and fourth lamps. Nothing seemed to be working. Owen's knees started to buckle as Matilda finally tried switching on the fourth lamp, then the second, and finally the first. There was a low rumble and a rustle. Then a compartment opened in the bank's ceiling, and a piece of paper floated down. Matilda reached out and snatched it as it fluttered past.

"This is it," she whispered in an excited voice. "We found the second piece of the map."

"Who's in here?" a deep, angry voice called out from the shadows. Matilda and Owen both froze.

"There must be night watchmen," Matilda whispered.

"Show yourselves!" the voice called out again.

"Let's get out of here!" Owen said as Matilda tried to quickly dismount his shoulders. But Owen's balance was off, and they both tumbled to the ground.

Just then, a rather large guard carrying a torch stormed past, looking in every direction but toward the ground.

"Come on," Owen whispered as he started crawling across the floor with Matilda right behind him. Once they saw the torchlight vanish at the far end of the bank, they jumped up and ran toward the door.

"That was close," Matilda said as she grabbed the door handle.

Just as the door started to swing open, a blaring alarm sounded. From the back of the bank, several torchlights appeared and started rushing toward Owen and Matilda.

"That's not good," Owen cried out. "Run!"

They made their way out the door and into the vacant street. The bank guards were not far behind.

"We'll never outrun them," Matilda said. "We need to find a place to hide."

The only thing on the empty street was

a carriage with two horses parked outside the front doors of the bank. In the front sat a driver slouching in his seat, his face concealed by the hood of a large cloak. When he saw Matilda and Owen running from the bank, he kicked the carriage door open and shouted, "Get in!"

Owen didn't know anyone on the island of Golden Harbor, but with the guards pouring out of the bank brandishing their giant swords, he felt like they had very little choice. Owen and Matilda had barely scrambled into the carriage when the coachman whipped the horses into a gallop and they took off down the dark street.

"Where are we going?" Owen asked the driver, once the bank guards were safely in the distance.

"To *The Lark*, of course," was the reply.

"Oh . . ." Owen was confused. "Um, how do you know we're headed there?"

A merry laugh escaped the coachman's lips, and he threw back the hood of his cloak, revealing a tumble of red hair. He wasn't a "he" at all.

"Morgan!" Matilda cried out. "How did you know we'd be at the bank? Were you following us?"

"Does it matter?" Owen asked. "I'm just glad she was there. Otherwise we'd be in jail by now."

"Humph." Matilda exhaled. "I guess."

Morgan let out another chuckle. "I saw you two buying that long coat this afternoon at the market and figured you were working on some type of disguise. So, how'd the heist go?"

Owen and Matilda shared an awkward look as the carriage pulled into the docks.

Chapter Nine

A Fern Grows in Bouffant Bay

"Pirates!" Billy shouted.

"Where?" Owen swung his head around and scanned the waters. The sun had just come up, and he'd been thinking about their next destination, Bouffant Bay. Owen had been so preoccupied with finding the map pieces, he'd almost forgotten about Captain Crawfish.

But there he was. His pirate ship was flying the Jolly Roger and had its cannons pushed forward, ready for action. It was closing in on *The Lark*.

"Bilge! Get Morgan!" Owen ordered.

"But the soup will burn," the cook protested.

"Tell her, anyway!" Owen bellowed. "We can always make more soup!"

"Aye," Bilge grumbled as he scurried belowdecks.

The loud crack of explosions filled the air.

"They're shooting at us!" Billy cried out. "What do we do?"

"This is not good," Owen said as he saw cannonballs heading their way. "Not good at all."

Billy screamed as a cannonball whizzed past his head and splashed down just inches from the side of *The Lark*.

"Full speed ahead," Morgan called out as she ran out onto the deck. "We've got the faster ship. As long as the wind is on our side that pirate ship shouldn't be able to gain on us."

"Yeah, but those cannonballs might," Matilda said. "If Crawfish sinks us, it doesn't matter how fast this ship of yours is."

Morgan shrugged. "Just keep your head down and I'll get us out of this. This isn't the first time I've had to outrun a pirate ship."

Cannonballs continued screaming past their heads as Owen and Matilda sat on the deck and tried to keep out of the way. Matilda's face was still red from arguing with Morgan.

"Why don't you like her?" Owen asked.

"There's something about her I just don't trust," Matilda replied. "And I don't like how smug she is. 'Oh, I have such a fast ship. Blah, blah, blah. Look how cool I am. Blah, blah, blah.'"

"Come on," Owen said. "She's not that bad. And she did save us at the bank."

"I don't care," Matilda replied. "I still don't trust her."

"Look!" Billy called out. "Crawfish is falling back!"

Owen and Matilda poked their heads over the side of the ship. A few final cannonballs were halfheartedly lobbed in their direction, but other than that, it appeared the pirate ship was giving up pursuit.

"I told you we'd outrun them," Morgan said.

"That and they don't want to get too close to the authorities at Bouffant Bay," Bilge noted.

"There's that, too," Morgan agreed.

Once they'd pulled into port, Owen and Matilda prepared to head into the town. Bouffant Bay appeared fairly pleasant, with lots of green ivy and large stone buildings. There did seem to be quite a few soldiers standing guard, probably due to Captain Crawfish.

"Guard your tongues and your hair," Bilge called after them as they headed up the dock. "You don't want people talking about what you're looking for, and this island is known for its outlandish barbers."

Owen turned and gave the old sailor a quizzical look.

"I wonder if he'll ever say anything helpful," Matilda said as they continued down the dock.

As they crossed into town, they discussed the next clue: *When ferns are your passion, you'll find you're in fashion. If things get too hot, you've found the right spot.*

"Looking for ferns, are ye?" a voice asked from the crowd. Stepping in front of them was a shifty-looking character with an eye patch and a rusty cutlass. "The name's Skinny Muldoon, but everyone just calls me Old Skinny. I can help you find anything you be lookin' for."

"Anything?" Owen asked.

Old Skinny nodded eagerly. "Shrimps, shoes, dancin' monkeys, whatever," he said. "And especially plants."

Owen looked at Matilda. "Well," he said to her, "it can't hurt to ask."

"I guess not," Matilda replied, although she didn't look convinced.

"Old Skinny, does this mean anything to you: 'When ferns are your passion, you'll find you're in fashion. If things get too hot, you've found the right spot'?"

"Of course, of course," Old Skinny said, his one eye shifting back and forth. "It means . . . ah . . . ah . . . it means, um . . ."

Owen and Matilda both gave him suspicious looks.

"Okay, so I don't know what it means," Old Skinny admitted. "But if it's ferns you be looking for, I can show you some."

"Great," Owen said.

"For a doubloon," Skinny added.

"Fine," Owen said as he pulled a coin from his pocket.

Old Skinny grabbed it from his hand and took off down the street. "Are you comin' or what?" he called back.

Matilda and Owen hurried after him. After several twisting turns, Old Skinny stopped in the middle of an old street. "Well, here we are," he announced.

"And where is 'here'?" Matilda asked.

"Why, Fern Way, of course," he said with pride as he waved his hand in the air.

Owen and Matilda looked up and down the street. It was full of old-looking buildings and shops. In front of each were rows and rows of potted ferns.

"Well, if you two need anything else, just ask anyone for Old Skinny," he said. "Everyone in Bouffant Bay knows how to find me."

"Thanks," Owen said as Old Skinny took off down the street.

"There must be hundreds of ferns," Matilda

said. "It's going to take us all day to search through every one of those pots."

Owen and Matilda spent the better part of the day looking at ferns without any ' ... Finally, they decided to take a break and get something to eat. Sitting in a small café, drinking root beer and eating sandwiches, Matilda suddenly stood up and pointed out the window.

"What is it?" Owen asked.

"There's a ladies' clothing store across the street, next to that bakery," she said.

"So?"

"So, it's all about fashion. And look at the address, 312 Fern Way. That's got to mean something," Matilda said.

Owen stuffed the rest of his sandwich into his mouth. "Let's check it out," he said after he'd washed the food down with a gulp of root beer.

The shop sold all kinds of stuff for the fashionable female, from lace petticoats to festooned hats.

"This is just clothes and things," Owen said. "I don't see any ferns."

"Look," Matilda said, jabbing him in the ribs.

There was a decorative fireplace at one end of the room with three carved panels showing some type of design. After taking a few steps closer, Owen realized the designs were actually meant to be ferns. "This is it," Owen said. "It's got to be."

"I bet it's like the bank, where there's a secret compartment," Matilda said.

Running their hands along the mantelpiece, they searched for a secret lever or a button or something. Owen tapped one of the carved panels. It sounded hollow. "Do you think we should just bust it open?" he asked.

Matilda rolled her eyes. "I really don't think smashing it will help."

Owen folded his arms. "Okay, fine. How do we get it open?"

"Let me think." Matilda chewed her lip. Suddenly, her eyes brightened. "Oh, I think I know." She stepped up to the fireplace. "The address of this building is three-one-two. Maybe that's got something to do with it." She reached forward and pressed on the third panel, then the first, then the second. There was the sound of creaking old wood, and then the panels started to slide, revealing a hidden compartment that contained a small wooden box. Matilda snatched the box from its hiding place and snapped it open. A huge smile spread across her face, and she gave Owen a nod.

"What are you two doing there?" a sales clerk demanded.

Matilda immediately hid the box up the sleeve of her jacket. "Nothing," she said. "Just shopping for something a little more fashionable than what I've got on."

"That won't be hard to do," the clerk replied with a condescending roll of her eyes.

"Actually"—Matilda wrinkled her nose— "there's nothing here I really like. It's all very last season." She turned to Owen and said, "Come on, Timothy. They have much nicer things on Golden Harbor." With that, the two of them scampered out of the shop.

"We've only got two pieces of the map left to find," Owen crowed as they made their way back to *The Lark*.

"What map?" Morgan asked, stepping out from a doorway where she'd been idling.

Owen and Matilda stared at the smuggler, wide-eyed. "The . . . um . . .," Owen tried to think.

"Uh . . . ," Matilda added. "Map of the town. We had a map of the town, but then some dog tore it to pieces, and we were just trying to paste it together again."

"Oh." Morgan nodded as if this explanation made perfect sense. "I think I have some paste in my cabin if you need it."

"How did you find us?" Owen asked.

"You can find anything in this town for a doubloon," she replied.

Owen and Matilda looked at each other.

"Old Skinny," they said in unison.

They all headed back to the docks together. "So, where to next?" Morgan asked.

"Gee, I don't know," Owen tried to sound casual. "I've always kind of wanted to visit Parrot Port. What do you think, Matilda?" he asked.

She shrugged. "Sounds good to me."

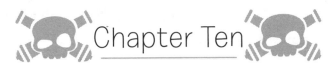

Chapter Ten

Dangers from the Deep

"We got to get out of here," Billy squeaked. "It's almost like Captain Crawfish knows exactly where *The Lark* is heading."

The tall masts of the pirate ship could be seen coming into view.

Morgan immediately began ordering her crew to take evasive action.

"I thought your ship was supposed to be stealthy," Matilda said.

"It is stealthy," Morgan snapped back at her. "It must have been you two running your mouths in town."

"I highly doubt that," Matilda replied.

Because *The Lark* was small and low in the water, Morgan was able to maneuver the ship behind a cay lined with palm trees. There they waited until Crawfish's sails had disappeared from sight.

Over the side of the ship, Bilge lowered a net into the water. "What are you doing?" Owen asked him.

"Looking to see what I can catch," the old sailor explained. "I have a hankering for sushi, and we'll just have to see what jumps in my net." A few minutes later, the old salt let out a cry of excitement.

"What is it?" Owen wanted to know.

"Calamari!" was the reply. "And lots of it."

Sure enough, there was a very large squid tangled in the sailor's net. It was the biggest squid Owen had ever seen and quite easily as tall as a very tall man.

"Help me haul her in," Bilge said, tugging at his net. "We're going to have a feast tonight."

But no one moved to help the old man.

"Hello?" he cried. "Trying to provide dinner here. With the biggest squid anyone of ye ever saw."

"That's not the biggest squid I ever saw," Billy said in a hushed voice.

The old man turned to glare at the boy. "Oh

really? Ye be telling me you've seen a bigger one?"

"Yes," Billy said, his voice trembling as the words left his mouth. "There's that one right behind you."

Bilge slowly turned, all the color draining from his face. It was true. The entire crew of *The Lark* was frozen in terror as a squid the size of a house swam toward them. The animal's giant eyes were red with rage. "Now *that's* some calamari," the old man whispered.

A huge tentacle from the squid crashed down in the water next to *The Lark* and began to wrap around the ship. "Man your posts," Morgan called to her crew. "We've got to get out of here!"

Another blow from an enormous tentacle knocked Billy into the water. "Help!" he shouted before another tentacle swept him up.

"It's going to eat him!" Bilge yelled.

"But squid don't eat little boys," Morgan insisted. "They eat shrimp."

"I don't think this one knows the difference," the old man countered.

Using his cutlass, Owen began hacking at the

net that held the smaller squid prisoner.

"What are you doing?" Bilge demanded. "It took me a whole year to weave that net."

"We've got to get this little squid loose, and I mean right now!" Owen shouted.

"Why?" Bilge asked. "So it can fight the bigger one?"

"No," Owen told him. "Because I think that's the mama and this is the baby."

As soon as the smaller squid was free from the net and began swimming away, the giant squid stopped thrashing. It even went so far as to release Billy, who swam to the boat and was grateful to be hauled aboard.

"That was good thinking," Matilda said as the mother and baby giant squid swam off toward the horizon. "Now let's get out of here before any other oversize angry mothers of the sea decide we're a threat."

Chapter Eleven

Runaround at Parrot Port

As they docked *The Lark* at Parrot Port, Billy couldn't help but exclaim, "Wow, this place is beautiful!" as he watched a flock of tropical birds swoop through the bright blue sky.

Bilge smacked his lips. "We might be having some parrot stew tonight."

Billy looked horrified, but Owen didn't have time to explain that the old sailor was probably just teasing.

"This place is a tropical paradise," Matilda said.

"Maybe we can hit the beach for a few hours before we go hunting for that final map piece," Owen joked.

"I can't believe that I forgot to pack my swimsuit," she replied with a smile.

"We should probably get going," Owen said,

his expression becoming serious. "Who knows what Crawfish is up to?"

Matilda nodded, and they headed toward the gangplank.

"So, what's the clue for Parrot Port again?" Matilda asked as they walked through town.

Owen replied, "'Birds of a feather guard the vast treasure. If you're ever at such a port of call, you'll have to make a feathered friend if you want any treasure at all.'"

"There are birds everywhere," Matilda said. "Where do we even start?"

"Let's make a feathered friend," Owen said as he walked over to a green-and-yellow parrot sitting on a fence post. "Hi, friend, what's your name?" Owen asked the bird as he reached out his hand in a friendly gesture.

The parrot let out a mean squawk, lunged forward, and bit Owen on the finger.

"Oww!" Owen cried out as he pulled his hand back. "These birds don't seem all that friendly."

"You just haven't found the right one," Matilda replied.

Owen turned to see Matilda standing with a red macaw parrot resting on her shoulder.

"Hello," the bird said to Matilda.

"Hello to you, parrot," she replied.

"'Birds of a feather,'" the parrot squawked. "'Feathered friend.'"

Owen's face lit up and he ran over to Matilda. "Do you know where the treasure is?" he asked the red parrot.

"Squawk! Jump in the sea, then come and find me," the bird screeched before flying away.

Matilda laughed. "I don't think the parrots like you very much."

"No, I don't think they do, either," Owen said. "Should we do what he said?"

"You mean jump in the sea?" Matilda asked.

"Yeah, he knew about 'birds of a feather' and 'feathered friend.' They're both parts of the clue."

"He's just a parrot," Matilda replied. "All he does is repeat what he hears. He must have heard us talking."

"I'm going to do what he said," Owen called back as he ran toward the ocean. "The clue said to listen to the parrot."

"The clue didn't say that at all," Matilda yelled after him, but it was too late. Owen was already halfway to the water.

Owen dove headfirst into the ocean. Popping up out of the warm water, he called out, "Okay, red bird, I've jumped in the water." He searched the sky for the parrot but couldn't see it anywhere. "I guess I have to find you."

Matilda stood at the water's edge and waited as Owen made his way to shore. "I think you're starting to lose it," she said.

"Maybe," he replied as he ran back toward town. "But maybe I'm right. C'mon, let's go find that parrot."

"Fine, but if we don't find that macaw in five minutes, we need to try something else," Matilda said as she followed after him.

Owen ran straight back to where they first saw the red parrot. Looking around, he started jumping up and down and waving his arms. "Here, parrot," he called out. "I jumped in the water like you asked; now tell me where the treasure is."

Matilda walked up beside him. "Look, I don't think that bird's coming back. I'm sure the clue means something else. Let's sit down and talk it through."

Owen stopped waving his arms and jumping.

"I was sure that I was right. I feel like a fool."

"Well, you did listen to a macaw that told you to jump into the ocean," she said. "You should feel a little foolish."

Owen smiled at her. "I guess. Let's get working on that clue."

Just then they heard a familiar squawk. Owen and Matilda looked up to see the red parrot perched above them on a thatched roof. The bird appeared very pleased to see Owen. It ruffled its feathers and said, "Squawk! To an old tower go, and find a pirate I know."

"Thanks, parrot," Owen said as the bird flew away. He then turned to Matilda, who stood quietly behind him. "So, who's the fool now?"

There was only one building in Parrot Port that had any type of tower. It looked like some kind of old fort that overlooked the bay.

"That must be it," Owen said as they made their way back down to the water. "Let's go see who's waiting for us up there."

"We should be careful," Matilda said. "We haven't had the best luck with pirates so far."

Pushing open an old wooden door, Owen peered in at a dark, cobwebbed staircase that led up into the tower. Matilda pushed her head in beside his. "This doesn't look safe," she said.

Owen pulled out his cutlass and started up the stairs. "Stay behind me."

At the top of the staircase, they could see sunlight coming from an open doorway. Cautiously making their way to the door, Owen peeked inside. Sitting in the corner of the tower was an elderly pirate relaxing in the sun.

A moment later, a shadow swept over the room as the red parrot flew in through the window and landed on the pirate's shoulder.

"'Feathered friend,'" the parrot squawked.

The old pirate leaped to his feet. He wobbled for a moment before grabbing hold of his chair. "What is it?" he called out. "Who's up here? Oh, it's you, my old friend," he said to the parrot.

"Um . . .," Owen said, not exactly sure what to do next.

"'Feathered friend,'" the bird repeated.

The old pirate turned his head to Owen. A look of relief fell over his face.

"Aye, ye've done it, lad. Me faithful Polly has directed you to me hiding spot," the pirate said drowsily. "For three generations now, my family has trained parrots to respond to certain words while we've guarded a great secret. I was thinking that I would have to pass the responsibility on to my son. But now I can relinquish our burden to you."

"Burden?" Owen wondered.

"Aye." The pirate nodded sagely. Reaching into his breast pocket, he pulled out a billfold, and from that billfold, he handed Owen a piece of paper. "I hope you can make better use of it than I."

Chapter Twelve

Return to Pirate Outpost

They returned to *The Lark* feeling triumphant. However, there was still one piece of the map left to find, and they knew it would be the most difficult to obtain. That piece was hidden somewhere back at Pirate Outpost.

"Are you sure you want to go with me to Pirate Outpost?" Owen asked. "I don't think that pirate with the gold tooth is going to be too pleased to see us again."

Matilda nodded. "I've come this far," she said. "We need to see this through together."

The sun began to set as Pirate Outpost came into sight on the horizon. From a distance, the whole island looked like one giant, foreboding stone skull. As the ship edged closer, Owen could see a bright light coming from the island.

"What's that?" he asked. "Is someone trying to signal us?"

"It looks more like a reflection," Matilda replied.

"It's nothing," Morgan said. "Happens every time we come here this late in the day. It's just the sunlight reflecting off the gold tooth in that giant skull."

Owen and Matilda looked at each other. "That's the gold tooth," he said. "Quick, Morgan, take us to it."

"No way," she said. "Those pirates love that tooth more than their own mothers."

Matilda pushed past Owen and stepped right up to Morgan. "You don't understand," she said. "We have to get to that tooth."

"You're right, I don't understand," Morgan replied. "And before we go one inch closer to that island, you two are going explain it all to me."

"I thought you didn't ask questions," Owen said.

"I don't, but if you're planning on stealing

that gold tooth, then I need to know," she said. "If those pirates even think we're up to something, this ship will be at the bottom of the harbor before we get to the docks."

Matilda's face reddened, but Owen stopped her before she said anything that would make their situation worse.

"I don't think we actually have to take the tooth," he said. "We just have to get something that might be hidden inside it."

"Another piece of your secret map?" Morgan asked.

Owen nodded.

"And does this map lead to a hidden treasure?"

Owen nodded again.

"And that hidden treasure contains my payment?"

Owen nodded a third time.

"Well, there's only one thing we can do," Morgan added with a mischievous smile. "Let's get you to that tooth."

They waited until the sun went down and then maneuvered *The Lark* into the mouth of the giant skull. As they moved below the gold tooth, Owen and Matilda tried to work up a plan to scale the skull's rock walls.

Morgan walked up behind them. "Those walls are as smooth as glass," she said. "There's no way you two are going to climb them."

"Well then, what do you suggest?" Matilda asked.

"If we can't get to the tooth," she replied, "then we should bring the tooth to us."

They all looked up at the giant piece of gold suspended above them.

"And how do we do that?" Owen asked. He and Matilda looked over at Morgan.

"Yeah. If this ship of yours had a cannon, we could blast it out," Matilda added.

Morgan thought for a minute. "I can get us a cannon. I'll need to go to the outpost, but I shouldn't be gone for too long."

"One of us needs to go with you," Matilda said as Morgan moved the ship out of the cave and to a nearby dock. "Now that you know our secret, I don't trust you out of our sight."

"Sorry," Owen added. "I have to agree with Matilda. There's too much at stake here. One of us should go."

"No dice," Morgan replied. "Those pirates don't like you. And if I show up with either of you, there's no way they'll sell me a cannon. Either it's just me, or it doesn't happen."

Owen and Matilda didn't see any way around it. "Fine," Owen said. "We'll just have to trust you."

"I should be back within the hour," Matilda said as she leaped from the dock. "Move *The Lark* back into the cave until I return."

"I don't like this one bit," Matilda said as soon as Morgan was out of earshot. "She could come back with a team of thugs and take the map pieces from us. And then where will we be?"

Owen was unsure. "I don't think she's that kind of person," he said. "She and her crew could have taken the pieces by now if they really wanted to. I think we have to trust her."

A while later, Owen saw several shadowy figures pushing something onto the dock. He could hear mumbled voices arguing through the night air, but he couldn't make out what they were saying. Eventually, there was some kind of exchange, and all but one of the people vanished back into the darkness. The remaining figure waved toward the cave, and *The Lark* began moving toward the dock.

As they moved out of the cave, Owen saw Morgan standing next to a small cannon on wheels. Alongside it was a small wooden box filled with cannonballs and gunpowder.

"It's not that big, but it will do the job," Morgan said as her crew loaded the cannon onto the ship.

"Why don't we just take the tooth and forget about the treasure?" Billy asked as he examined the cannon.

Matilda furrowed her brow. "I think we should try to take the tooth *and* get the treasure. I mean, it's probably gold they took from Fort Ridley anyway."

"That gold belongs to the pirates of this island," Morgan replied. "We're going to be in big enough trouble for blasting it out of the cave. But if we try to steal it, they won't stop until they have all our heads."

Owen knew she was right. "Let's just get the map piece and get out of here."

Morgan packed the cannon with gunpowder and a cannonball and aimed it at the gold tooth. Below the tooth, Bilge and Billy stretched out a fishing net to catch it when it fell. Owen and Matilda grabbed hold, too. The tooth looked heavy.

"Ready?" Morgan asked as she lit a match. Everyone nodded, and she lit the fuse. After a few seconds' delay, there was a loud *BOOM*!

The cave walls shook, and the blast hit the giant skull square in the tooth. Chunks of rock broke free and sprayed out of the cave. After the noise faded and the dust settled, Owen looked up to see the gold tooth starting to slip from the mouth of the skull. "Okay, here it comes!" he shouted.

The tooth came free and plunged toward the deck. Bilge and Billy hurriedly tugged the net in one direction, while Matilda and Owen pulled it tight the other way. The giant hunk of gold crashed down on the net, bounced once, and then landed on the deck of *The Lark*.

Matilda and Owen dropped the net and ran over to the tooth.

"Hurry up and find that map piece," Morgan said. "We need to get the gold tooth onto the dock before those pirates get down here."

Owen turned the tooth over and found a small metal plate on its top. He pressed the plate, and a spring-loaded door opened. Inside was a rolled-up piece of parchment.

"Here it is," he called out. "I can't believe it. This is the final piece of the map."

The Lark moved out of the cave and slowed ever so slightly as it came to the small dock. As it passed by, Owen, Matilda, and Bilge hoisted the tooth and tossed it to shore.

"Get us out of here as fast as you can!" Owen yelled. In the distance, he could see dozens of angry pirates rushing toward the dock. Their swords were glistening in the moonlight.

Chapter Thirteen

The Missing Piece

"I can't believe we did it," Billy said as they huddled together belowdecks. "I can't believe we found all the pieces."

Matilda and Owen exchanged excited looks as they laid the map pieces out on the table.

"Okay, let's see what we have here." Matilda stooped over the table to assemble the scraps of paper. "Hmmm . . .," she said with a frown.

"What?" Owen did not like the expression on her face. It made him nervous.

"I hate to say it, but I think we're missing a piece."

"What?" Owen exclaimed, bending over to double-check her work. "We can't be. We went to all the islands. We followed all the clues."

"Aye, she's right," Bilge said. "There looks to be a wide band of parchment missing from the map. We not be findin' the location of the treasure without that."

"Great," Morgan said. "I have every pirate in the seas after this ship, and I'm not even going to get paid."

"We must have overlooked something," Matilda said.

Owen kept looking at the map, desperate for any clue about the missing section. *Does that drawing of a wavy line indicate an island, or does it have something to do with the stars?* he wondered. *Why is half the illustration of the compass missing?*

He pulled his cutlass from its scabbard and slapped it down on the table. Along the side of the blade a portion of an ornate compass with ships, islands, and longitudinal marks lined up with the missing portion of the map.

"That's it!" Matilda shouted. "Governor Ridley must have given the last piece of the map to Captain Nathaniel Christopher to guarantee that even if someone found all the other map pieces, they couldn't get to the treasure. That's why the sword has been passed down from generation to generation, Owen. Your family has been the guardian of Fort Ridley's treasure."

"Wow," Owen said. "I can't believe I had the final piece all along."

"Yeah, that's great!" Morgan said as she rubbed her hands together. "So let's go get my payment. Where are we headed?"

Bilge looked up from the map. "Says the island's called Skullduggery."

It took quite a few hours, but once they found the island, it was easy to understand why its location wasn't noted on many maps. The whole area was shrouded in a thick mist, and the island itself was little bigger than *The Lark*.

"At least with a small island, there aren't that many places to dig," Billy said as he stood on deck with a shovel in his hand.

"Do you guys want any help?" Morgan asked as Owen and Matilda prepared to disembark the ship.

"We should be fine." Owen shook his head as

he grabbed the shovel from Billy. "There's not a lot of ground to cover."

"We'll signal if we need you," Matilda added.

There wasn't much on the island besides a single palm tree sticking out of its center. On the opposite end was a slight gully. "This looks like a good place to start digging," Owen said.

A while later, Owen was down inside a deep ditch, digging.

"Do you think this is the right place?" Matilda asked.

Just then Owen's shovel hit something that sounded like wood. He furiously started digging away at the dirt around it. After a short while, he unearthed a large wooden chest.

"I can't wait to find out what's inside," Owen said.

"Me too," Matilda added. "Let's open it now."

Using the blade of the shovel, Owen struck the lock. It was rusty with age and broke quite easily. Holding his breath, he undid the latches and flung back the lid.

There, sparkling in the afternoon sun, was a

huge stack of doubloons, jewel-encrusted chalices, ornate crowns, piles of pearls, and rings bearing giant diamonds, emeralds, and rubies.

"Wow," was all Owen could say as his eyes took in all the glittering treasure. "This is . . . just wow." After a few more moments of staring, he picked up a diamond-and-ruby-encrusted tiara and called to Matilda. "Hey, why don't you try this on?"

His joke was met with silence.

"Matilda?" he called to her. He stood up and peeped out of the hole. She wasn't there.

Owen started climbing out, but he didn't get very far before he was knocked to the ground by a blow to the head. "Ouch," he said, pressing a hand to his skull where a lump was already starting to form. Standing over the treasure was none other than Captain Crawfish.

Chapter Fourteen

X Marks the Spot

The pirate stared down at Owen with his one good eye. A wide, villainous smile crept across his face. "I thought you'd never lead me to this treasure," he said in a deep, booming voice. "But you turned out to be every bit as clever as I'd heard."

Owen leaped to his feet and went to pull out his cutlass.

"I wouldn't do that," Crawfish said, stepping aside to reveal several mean-looking pirates holding Matilda, Billy, and Bilge. Owen's three friends were gagged and had their hands tied. "Unless you want something bad to happen to your friends."

Owen moved his hand away from his sword.

"Good," Crawfish said. "Now help my men get that treasure chest out of that hole."

"And then what are you going to do with us?" Owen asked.

"Well," Crawfish replied, "if you do everything I say, then I'll let you and your friends live. I'm only here for the treasure."

"I have one more question: How do you keep finding us?" Owen asked. "You seem to know everywhere we go."

"I have a sixth sense for these things," the pirate told him.

The pirates all laughed.

"Yeah," Crawfish added, "and her name is Morgan."

"What?" Owen couldn't believe it. He glanced at Matilda, who gave him an "I told you so" look.

"I'm afraid it's true," Morgan said as she stepped out from behind the other pirates. "And for what it's worth, I'm sorry."

"But why?" he asked her. "I thought we were friends."

"I have my reasons," she told him. "You have your way of doing things, and I have mine."

At that moment, Matilda managed to kick

one of her captors in the shin and spit out her gag. "You traitor! You've ruined everything!"

Owen couldn't look at Morgan any longer. He turned his attention to the pirates who'd started to lift the chest out of the hole. With his help, they were able to get it up and onto Crawfish's ship. Once he was onboard, Owen saw Captain MacCullen, along with the crew of *The Guppy* and several other captured sailors from Fort Ridley, chained to the deck. He and MacCullen shared a brief look, acknowledging their mutual defeat. Then, with the treasure secure, two pirates lifted Owen up and tossed him overboard.

This made Crawfish laugh so hard he had to hold his belly. He, Morgan, and the other pirates started up the gangplank, leaving Matilda, Billy, and Bilge on the island. "I'm afraid you and your little friends will have to stay here," he called to Owen, who struggled to swim to shore.

"Here?" Billy cried out. "You can't leave us here."

Crawfish turned to face the boy. "As a pirate, you can see how foolish it would be for me to sail into a port and drop off a few passengers. You might do something stupid, like turn me in."

"What are we supposed to do?" Matilda asked.

The pirate shrugged. "Wait for the mist to clear."

Crawfish's ship sailed away from Skullduggery Island. *The Lark* followed close behind.

"It was nice doing business with you, Crawfish," Morgan said on the deck of Crawfish's ship as the pirate inspected the treasure. "I suppose you'll be heading out now that I've made good on our agreement."

"Ah, yes. Our agreement," the pirate captain said, pulling

at some of the hairs on his chin. "What was it again? Refresh my memory."

Morgan ground her teeth with annoyance, but she managed to hold her temper. "We agreed that if I befriended the Christopher boy and led you to the treasure, you'd sail away from these waters, never to return," she said.

"Ah, yes." The pirate nodded. "I do remember that as our agreement. And I shall stick to my word, but for one thing."

"What's that?" Morgan asked, dreading his reply.

"First I'm going to flatten Fort Ridley to make sure no one else gets any ideas about challenging Captain Crawfish." He turned to his guards and shouted, "Seize her!"

But it was too late; Morgan had anticipated the captain's betrayal. She kicked his peg leg, knocking him off balance. Crawfish swung at her with his massive arm, but Morgan ducked under it and dove into the water.

She swam for *The Lark*, where her crew was ready and waiting. The pirate's boat was big and well armed, but it wasn't built for speed. Morgan's ship disappeared over the horizon before the pirates could even get underway.

"No matter." Crawfish chuckled to himself. "Even if she does try to warn her hometown, who is going to believe the word of a smuggler?" He flashed a wicked grin. "That's why it pays to do business with thieves."

Turning to his first mate, Captain Crawfish ordered, "Set a course for Fort Ridley."

Meanwhile, Owen sat on the sandy beach of Skullduggery Island. "I'm a failure," he said to the others. "I let down my family, I let down Fort Ridley, and I let down the legacy of the Christophers."

"It's not your fault," Matilda said as she sat down next to him.

Owen threw a rock into the water. "It's entirely my fault," he said. "I should have listened to you. You told me not to trust Morgan, and I didn't listen."

Matilda shrugged her shoulders.

"If I had listened, we wouldn't be here now," he added. "We'd be halfway back to Fort Ridley with a hundred ships to stop Crawfish."

"It's still not too late to stop him," a familiar voice called out.

Everyone whipped their heads around to see Morgan and her crew heading toward them.

"What are you doing back here?" Owen demanded. "There's nothing left for you to take."

"Look," Morgan said, not quite sure how to begin, "I know I screwed up."

"Screwed up? You sold us out!" Matilda yelled at her.

"But please hear me out," she replied. "It's true that Crawfish hired me to keep an eye on you. We made a deal: I help him steal the treasure, and then he leaves Fort Ridley forever."

"And how did that work out for you?" Owen asked. "Did the pirate keep his word?"

"No," Morgan said. "That's why I need your help. Fort Ridley needs your help."

Owen stood up and finally faced her. "Why should I? You've been lying to us this entire time."

"I know," Morgan said. "But I'm not lying now. Yeah, I let Crawfish have the treasure, but then he stabbed me in the back. He's on his way to Fort Ridley right now to demolish the town."

"I hate her more than you do," Matilda said to Owen. "But if there's any chance we can stop Crawfish and save our home, I say we go for it."

Owen nodded in agreement. "Fine," he said to Morgan. "But I'm in charge. You and your crew listen to me."

Chapter Fifteen

The Final Showdown

Fog began to roll in as *The Lark* raced toward Fort Ridley. There wasn't enough time to warn the governor about the attack, so they needed to come up with a plan to stop Crawfish before he reached the island.

Though most ships would have found it impossible to navigate, Morgan and her crew were skilled at moving through the dark and fog. Owen hoped that Captain Crawfish had run into the bad weather as well.

"The only advantage we have is the element of surprise," Owen said to Morgan. "If we can sneak up next to Crawfish's ship, I bet we could board without him knowing it."

"And then what?" Morgan replied. "They have us outnumbered ten to one."

"If we can release Captain MacCullen and

the others, we might have a chance," he said. "We could overwhelm them before they know what's happening."

"That sounds like a horrible plan," Morgan said. "But you're in charge, right?"

"That's right," Owen said. "Tell your crew to prepare for the ambush."

Just as Owen had hoped, the fog had brought Crawfish's ship to a standstill.

"I guess luck is on our side," Morgan said under her breath as she navigated *The Lark* alongside the pirate ship.

"Are you sure you want to do this?" Matilda whispered to Owen.

"This is our only chance to stop Crawfish," Owen replied. "I don't see that we have a choice."

"Fine," she said. "But I'm coming with you."

Before he could object, Billy stepped up, wooden sword in hand. "Me too," he said. "We can't let you go over there alone."

"I can't let you two risk your lives," Owen

said. "I got us into this mess; I need to be the one to get us out."

"You're not going to stop us," Matilda said, securing a cutlass to her belt.

Owen knew he had no choice; they weren't going to back down. "All right then," he said. "Let's get going. Morgan, you know the plan, right? Once we get up those ropes"—he pointed to several ropes hanging off the side of Crawfish's ship—"you fire a cannonball at the opposite deck. That should distract them long enough for us to free MacCullen and the others."

Once they were up the ropes and against the side of the pirate ship, Owen gave Morgan the signal, and then . . .

BOOM!

"What was that?" someone from Crawfish's ship shouted as a cannonball whizzed through the fog.

"Our ship is under attack!" Owen heard Captain Crawfish call from belowdecks.

While the pirates were still in a state of
confusion, Owen and the others slipped over the
side of the ship and ducked into the shadows.

Over the commotion, Owen heard a scraping sound. It was getting closer. He knew right away that it was Crawfish's peg leg dragging along the ship's deck.

"Get out here, you runt," the pirate called out. "I know you're behind this."

Owen leaped out of the shadows, his cutlass drawn and ready.

"What do you think you're doing?" Crawfish said with a chuckle.

"I'm taking command of your ship," Owen said. "Now drop your weapon and call off your men."

Captain Crawfish let out a laugh that shook the timbers of his ship. "And just how do you be planning to do that?" the pirate asked.

"I'm going to fight you," Owen said. "And when I win, you'll surrender."

"What happens when you lose?" Crawfish asked. "Because you will lose."

"I won't lose," Owen said.

"And what makes you think that?" the pirate wanted to know.

"Because," Owen said, a wide smile spreading across his face as Captain MacCullen and dozens of other armed and angry men and women filled in behind him, "while we were talking, my shipmates freed all your prisoners."

"It's going to take more than a bunch of old sailors and farmers to defeat me," Crawfish said as he lunged at Owen with his sword. Around him, a swarm of angry pirates charged at MacCullen and the others.

Owen swung his cutlass and blocked Crawfish's attack, but the power of the blow knocked him back. After regaining his footing, he charged at Crawfish. The much bigger pirate easily deflected his attack.

"Give it up, kid," Crawfish said as he swung at Owen again, just missing him.

"Never!" Owen yelled back as he ducked behind the mast, using it to block the pirate's attacks.

Matilda and Billy ran up next to him, their swords drawn. "Looks like you could use a little help," she said.

"That's an understatement," he replied. "Crawfish is a lot tougher than he looks. And he looks *really* tough."

"If we all charge at the same time, we might have a chance to overpower him," Matilda said.

"I have a better plan," Owen said. "Billy, go get some rope. Matilda, remember how we got past that one pirate with the scar on his face?"

"I remember it not ending all that well," she replied.

Just then, a pirate came up from behind and kicked Matilda in the side, sending her flying. Owen spun around and sliced his cutlass at the pirate. But the pirate was quick and scurried up the ship's mast. Owen climbed up after him.

Once at the top, the pirate stomped his boot down on Owen's hand. Owen tried to hold on as best he could. The pirate brought his foot down again, but this time Owen was able to grab hold of his ankle. The pirate struggled to break free, but Owen wouldn't let go. As the pirate went to take out his sword, Owen pulled as hard as he could, yanking the pirate off the mast and sending him into the ocean below.

From the mast, Owen hunted the ship for Crawfish. Once he spied him, Owen quickly climbed down and found Billy and Matilda waiting for him. They tied a rope around Billy's waist and sent him off after Crawfish. Matilda followed closely behind him.

Owen pushed his way through the fight and headed straight for Crawfish. The pirate spotted him approaching and knocked aside the sailor he was fighting.

"Give it up, Crawfish," Owen said. "We've got you beat."

Crawfish looked around and laughed. "You're losing," he said. "Your men are all but defeated."

"Yeah, but I'm not," Owen said. "Come and get me."

Crawfish roared and charged at Owen. After two steps, he felt something tug on his one good leg. He looked down and realized that Billy and Matilda had caught his legs in the rope. He tried to stop himself from tumbling over, but it was too late. The mighty pirate toppled over, smacking the deck with a loud thud. All the pirates stopped fighting and watched as their leader crumpled to the ground.

Owen rushed forward and kicked the cutlass out of Crawfish's hand. The pirate struggled to get up on his one good leg, but Billy charged and pointed his wooden blade at the pirate's throat. Owen and Matilda stood right behind him. Crawfish knew he'd been defeated.

"I surrender," the captain blurted out.

"What was that?" Owen asked.

"I surrender!" the captain yelled.

Chapter Sixteen

Celebration

"Pirates!" a guard yelled, pointing toward the harbor.

In the distance, he saw two ships headed toward Fort Ridley: one a mighty pirate ship that was easily recognizable as Captain Crawfish's, the other a smaller, sleeker ship.

The governor and Jeeves headed down to the docks. By their side was a dashing man in a naval uniform.

"It doesn't look like MacCullen and your son were able to pull it off," Jeeves said to the naval officer.

"My son's a Christopher," the man replied. "It's best not to count him out too soon."

"Unless they show up with a fleet of ships in the next five minutes, I think I'm going to have to agree with Jeeves," Governor Roland said.

Captain Christopher, who had just returned to the island, stepped up to the edge of the docks. "I don't think they're here to attack," he said. "It just doesn't feel right."

Jeeves scoffed. "I say we get to safety and hope they don't find us," he said.

"You can hide," Captain Christopher said. "But I'm staying right here."

Governor Roland agreed. "We're staying. If this is Fort Ridley's last stand, this is where I need to be."

"Look," Captain Christopher said, pointing at the ships. "They don't even have their cannons run out. They're not prepared to attack. If you ask me"—he paused to brush a bit of dust from the sleeve of his naval jacket—"it looks like they're planning to dock."

"That's ridiculous!" Jeeves shouted. "They're obviously planning to flatten Fort Ridley. We should retreat to the farthest end of the island."

"No." The governor put a hand on his assistant's arm. "He's right. The cannons haven't been pushed forward so they can be used. They're not planning an assault."

"And look." The captain nodded toward the ship. "They're not flying the Jolly Roger."

"MacCullen must have done it," Governor Roland said. "He must have defeated Captain Crawfish and captured his ship."

The entire town broke out in celebration. Everyone rushed to the harbor to welcome the returning heroes.

Once Crawfish's ship had docked, with *The Lark* moored right next to it, the governor and Captain Christopher stepped forward to greet the heroic crew. First down the gangplank was Captain MacCullen, who was met with handshakes and pats on the back. Next was Matilda, who stopped in front of her father. "We will talk about this," he said as he gave her a giant hug. "But today we celebrate."

The crowd let out a collective gasp as Captain Crawfish stepped off the ship. His hands were manacled together and connected to a long chain.

The other end of the chain was held by Owen, who came around the side of the captured pirate and led him down the gangplank. Bilge and Billy trailed not far behind.

The two Christophers exchanged a brief nod before Governor Roland spoke up. "Captain MacCullen, all of Fort Ridley is in your debt. You have finally freed us of this horrible scourge."

"Well, ahh," MacCullen said, his face turning a bit red. "As much as I'd like to take credit for this feat, all the glory goes to the Christopher lad and your wee lass. I've been chained up on this here ship since before we hit the first port. And I rightly think I'd still be there if it weren't for those two."

"Is this true?" the governor asked Matilda.

She nodded. "It was Owen, really," she said. "He's the one who led us to the pieces of the treasure map. And it was his plan to capture Captain Crawfish. None of this would have happened without him."

"I guess you were right," the governor said to Captain Christopher. "Your son is a Christopher."

"Yes, he is," he agreed and smiled toward his son.

"This story is preposterous," Jeeves insisted. "You can't expect us to believe that Captain Crawfish was captured by some little kids."

"Hey," Morgan said, stepping through the crowd. "I know you." She pointed an accusing finger at Jeeves. "You're Captain Crawfish's guy. You're the one who hired me."

"You're in league with the pirates?" Matilda called out. "You've worked for our family for years."

"Jeeves, tell me this isn't true," Governor Roland said.

Jeeves only shrugged. "What did you expect me to do, just let you give away the treasure? Maybe the pirates would be gone, but we'd have nothing, just an old burned-out town. With my cut of the treasure I could have lived like a king on some faraway island."

"Well, now you're going to jail," the governor said as some soldiers stepped forward and clapped the traitor in irons.

Fort Ridley was finally free of the tyranny of Captain Crawfish and his dreaded crew. It was time to celebrate. An inventory of the pirate ship revealed not only the immense Fort Ridley treasure, but most of the food, money, and belongings that had been pillaged from the town.

At the pier, a huge party was underway. Billy

had his wooden sword out and was telling anyone who would listen about how he fought off a giant squid and then captured Captain Crawfish. Bilge was back up on his watchtower, cooking away and staring off at Captain Crawfish's ship, which the town had decided to sink in the harbor. Below, Morgan stood awkwardly with what appeared to be her family. It was clear that she was itching to be back out on the water.

Matilda pulled her father away from the celebration. She couldn't remember the last time she saw him this happy. "I'm sorry I disobeyed you," she said. "I just couldn't stand the thought of staying home while Owen and the others helped hunt him down."

"That's all right, my dear," the governor said, patting her affectionately on the head. "I'm just glad you're not injured or harmed in any way. I suppose if you want to join the navy so badly that you're willing to run away to do it, I should encourage you to pursue your dream."

"Thank you." She leaned in and kissed him on the cheek.

"Although, after the navy," he added, "you could still be governor someday."

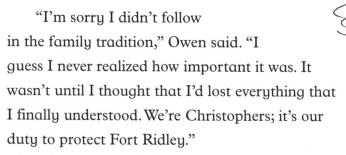

Owen and his father stood on the edge of the pier and watched the pirate ship slowly sink into the harbor.

"I'm sorry I didn't follow in the family tradition," Owen said. "I guess I never realized how important it was. It wasn't until I thought that I'd lost everything that I finally understood. We're Christophers; it's our duty to protect Fort Ridley."

"And I should have been more supportive," his father said. "I'm very proud of you, you know. It took a lot of courage to do what you did. And if you want to continue in the air service, that's fine with me."

"I think I'll stay in Fort Ridley for a while,"

Owen said. "They can probably use some help
rebuilding their navy. And who knows, maybe
they'll make me a captain one day."

Turn the page for a sneak preview of

Poptropica ®

ASTRO-KNIGHTS
ISLAND

available now!

Chapter One

Strange Disks in the Sky

Cock-a-doodle-doo!

Simon Cobb groaned at the sound of the rooster's loud morning crow.

If he had a pillow, he would have pulled it over his head, rolled over, and gone back to sleep. But the young stable boy slept on a thin mattress stuffed with straw, without a pillow or even a blanket. Besides, he didn't want to be late for work. That always put Edmund, the stable master, in a bad mood—and working in the stable was bad enough without Edmund stomping around.

He yawned and stood up, brushing a strand of brown hair from his eyes. The rooster strutted through the hut's open door and stared at Simon with accusing yellow eyes.

"Give me a break," Simon told the rooster. "The sun's not even up all the way."

A red-haired girl poked her head inside the hut. "Aren't you up yet, Simon?" asked Alice.

"It's not even daytime yet," Simon protested. "Anyway, why aren't you in the Castle?" Simon didn't know much about Alice's job in the Castle as a scullery maid, but he knew she had to be up even earlier than he did to help make breakfast for everyone in the royal court.

"I snuck out," she said, stepping inside. Her green eyes were shining. "I thought you'd want to know—the knights are riding out today!"

The news jolted Simon awake. Nothing much exciting happened out in the stables, but he always loved it when the knights came. Sir Pelleas, Sir Cador, and Sir Gawain were the superstars of Arturus. They were tall and strong, and they lived exciting lives, protecting the kingdom from danger.

Simon had been eagerly awaiting their next visit to the stables. He hoped to impress them so that one of them might make him a squire. Then he'd be able to leave the muck and horse manure behind and travel with the knights, helping them— and maybe even riding his own horse.

"They're riding out? Where?" Simon asked. He ran past Alice to the water bucket outside and splashed cold water on his face. The hut didn't have a mirror, so he gazed at his reflection in the water. He scrubbed a patch of dirt off his cheek and used some more water to smooth down a lock of hair sticking up on top of his head.

Alice shook her head. "Are you actually trying to impress them?"

"Just watch. I'm going to be a squire someday," he said confidently. "I'm not going to spend my whole life mucking out stables. I'm going to have a horse of my own."

"Well, you'd better let me ride it, then," Alice said. "I never get to do anything fun."

She thrust a hunk of bread and a hard-boiled egg into his hands.

"From the kitchens," she said. "Those royals have more food than they need."

"Thanks," Simon said.

His friend grinned. "No problem. Good luck impressing the knights! I'd better get back before they figure out I'm gone."